DON'T TALK
TO STRANGERS!

Veronika Martenova Charles

Illustrated by David Parkins

Tundra Books

Published in Canada by Tundra Books,
a division of Random House of Canada Limited, a Penguin Random House Company

Published in the United States by Tundra Books of Northern New York,
a division of Random House of Canada Limited, a Penguin Random House Company

Library of Congress Control Number: 2007943131

Library and Archives Canada Cataloguing in Publication

Charles, Veronika Martenova
    Don't talk to strangers! / Veronika Martenova Charles ; illustrated by David Parkins.

(Easy-to-read spooky tales)
ISBN 978-0-88776-847-7

1. Horror tales, Canadian (English). 2. Children's stories, Canadian (English).
I. Parkins, David II. Title. III. Series: Charles, Veronika Martenova. Easy-to-read
spooky tales.

PS8555.H42242D67 2008   jC813'.54   C2007–907591–6

**ONTARIO ARTS COUNCIL
CONSEIL DES ARTS DE L'ONTARIO**

We acknowledge the financial support of the Government of Canada through the Book
Publishing Industry Development Program (BPIDP) and that of the Government of
Ontario through the Ontario Media Development Corporation's Ontario Book Initiative.
We further acknowledge the support of the Canada Council for the Arts and the Ontario
Arts Council for our publishing program.

Printed and bound in Canada

www.penguinrandomhouse.ca

4 5 6   17 16 15

CONTENTS

IN THE PARK
PART 1

"I've got a new ball,"

I told Leon and Marcos.

"Let's go to the park

and play catch."

The park was almost empty.

There was only a man and a dog.

Leon, Marcos, and I played,

and the dog chased the ball.

The man watched us play,

but then he left the park.

"Look!" said Leon.

"The dog is still here.

The man left him behind."

"Maybe it's not his dog," I said.

"So, whose is it?" asked Marcos.

"It could be lost," I answered.

"Let's go and ask some people

if they know the dog.

Maybe they will recognize him

and take him to his owners."

"I'm not asking," said Leon.

"My mom always says

'Don't talk to strangers!'

And then she tells me a story

about Butterball."

"I have an idea," said Marcos.

"We could stay here with the dog

until the owner comes for him.

Then Leon can tell us the story

about Butterball."

"All right," Leon and I agreed.

★

BUTTERBALL

(Leon's Story)

Once there was a little boy

called Butterball

who lived with his mother

in a house in the woods.

One day, their dog began barking.

"Butterball," said the mother,

"go and see who is coming."

Butterball looked,

came back, and said,

"A stranger is coming

with her head under her arm

and a sack on her back."

Butterball's mother said,

"Don't talk to that stranger.

It must be a troll!

Run and hide!"

The troll came to the door.

"Good day!" she said.

"Is Butterball home today?"

"No, he's not," the mother said,

and she closed the door.

"That's too bad," the troll said.

"I've got a present for him –

a little silver knife."

"Here I am!" said Butterball,

who was listening.

He came out from under a bush.

"My back aches," said the troll.

"You'll have to get in the sack

and pull out the knife yourself."

When Butterball crawled in,

the troll tied the sack,

and carried it into the woods.

Soon she got tired,

so she lay down for a nap.

Butterball found the knife,

cut a hole in the sack,

and jumped out.

Then he ran home to his mother.

When the troll woke up

and found Butterball gone,

she was very angry.

The next day,

the troll came back.

"Good day," said the troll.

"Is Butterball home today?"

"No, he's not," said his mother,

and she went into the house.

"Too bad," called the troll.

"I had a silver spoon for him."

"Here I am!" said Butterball,

and he came out of hiding.

He climbed into the sack

to get the silver spoon.

The troll closed it and left.

But this time, she didn't stop.

She went all the way home.

There, she said to her daughter,

"Cook what's in the sack!

I'm going to wash in the river."

The daughter boiled some water,

and she opened the sack.

"Hello, Auntie!" said Butterball.

The daughter was confused.

Was the boy her nephew?

Then, she shouldn't cook him.

"I see some bugs in your hair,"

Butterball said.

"Please pick them out for me!"

the daughter said,

putting her head on the table.

Butterball threw the sack

over her head, and ran back home

to his mother. He never spoke

to strangers again.

"That's a scary story," I said.

A man was coming in the park.

"Maybe that's the owner,

coming to get the dog," I said.

But the man ignored us

and the dog didn't budge.

"Marcos, go and ask the man

if he knows the dog," said Leon.

"I'm not asking," said Marcos.

"He looks kind of strange –

like one of the people

from the story I've heard."

"Tell us the story!" I said.

THE LOST DOG

(Marcos' Story)

One evening,

Ben went to the corner store

to buy a bag of chips.

He took his dog with him.

Ben tied the dog's leash

to a post in front of the store

and went inside.

When Ben came out of the store,

his dog was not there.

Ben called him,

but he did not come.

Ben did not know what to do.

There was a man on the street

coming toward him.

"Excuse me," said Ben,

"but did you see my dog?"

"What did he look like?"

asked the man.

"He had big, black pointed ears,"

said Ben.

"Did they look like these?"

The man showed Ben his ears.

They were big,

black, and pointed.

Ben ran away.

Soon he met another man.

"Excuse me," said Ben,

"but did you see my dog?"

"What did he look like?"

asked this other man.

"He had huge eyes," said Ben.

"Did they look like these?"

The man took off his sunglasses.

He had eyes like pancakes

that covered half of his face.

Ben got scared and ran.

He almost bumped into a woman,

standing on the sidewalk.

"What's your hurry?"

the woman asked.

"I'm looking for my dog,"

said Ben.

"What did he look like?"

asked the woman.

"One of his paws was missing,"

answered Ben.

"Were they paws like these?"

asked the woman.

She grabbed Ben's shoulders.

Instead of hands,

she had enormous tiger paws.

Ben tore himself away from her

and ran all the way home.

When he got to his house,

he found his dog,

waiting for him.

★   ★   ★

"Wow, I'm scared," giggled Leon.

"I know a story about a stranger

who looked totally normal,

but she was a witch," I said.

"Shall I tell you?"

"Yes," said Leon and Marcos.

"Hurry. I'm going home soon,"

added Leon.

★

35

THE COUSIN

(My Story)

Jamal and Salma

were brother and sister.

Their parents died,

so they were always hungry

and looking for food.

One day, Jamal decided to go

to the countryside

and see if he could earn money

by working in the fields.

But no matter how much he asked,

no one offered him any work.

On the way back home,

he met an old woman.

"Where have you been?" she asked.

So, Jamal told her everything.

"Bring your sister and come live

with me," said the woman.

"You can share my wealth."

"Who are you?" asked Jamal.

"Your cousin," said the woman.

"I'm old and alone.

I would enjoy your company."

Jamal couldn't believe his luck,

so he ran to tell his sister.

That evening, Jamal and Salma

left town with the woman,

who took them to her house.

She fed them a big dinner.

When the woman went to the barn

to get some milk,

Salma followed,

thinking she might help.

But as she got close,

Salma heard the woman

talking to her cow.

"Tomorrow I will eat my guests,"

she said.

The cow mooed,

as if to say "No. No, no!"

Salma did not wait any longer.

She ran back to the house

to tell her brother.

"We must leave at once," she said.

"The woman plans to eat us!"

"Are you crazy?" said Jamal.

"You must have heard wrong.

Look how generous and kind

she has been!"

But Salma was scared,

and did not sleep all night.

In the morning, Salma followed

the woman to the barn again.

Again, she heard her say,

"Today, I will eat my guests."

And the cow mooed, as if to say

"No. No, no!"

Salma did not wait any longer.

She ran to her brother and said,

"Let's go now! This instant!"

But Jamal wouldn't listen.

"What's wrong with you?"

asked Salma.

"Stay if you like, but I'm leaving."

When the old woman returned,

she found only Jamal.

She locked the door, screeching,

"I'm not your cousin. I'm a witch!

And I love to eat the fools

who come into my house."

She pulled a big metal file

out of her pocket

and began to sharpen her teeth.

"Now, tell me. What part of you

should I eat first?"

Jamal shivered.

"Salma knew this would happen,

but I didn't listen," he said.

Then, Jamal had an idea. . . .

IN THE PARK

PART 2

"I have to go home," said Leon.

"I don't think anyone is coming

for the dog."

"Bye dog!" we said.

We started walking,

but the dog followed us.

"Let's take him home.

We can ask my mom what to do,"

said Leon.

When we got to Leon's house,

his mom was not there.

She had left a note:

I'll be back soon.

We gave the dog some cat food

and a bowl of water to drink.

"I was thinking," said Leon,

"What if we put the dog

on a leash and see if maybe

he'll lead us to his house."

"It's worth a try," said Marcos.

We made a leash out of rope

and put it on the dog.

The dog started pulling us along

and we followed him.

He was leading us back,

toward the park!

There were a few houses near

the park, and the dog stopped

in front of one of them.

"We can't just leave him

on the porch," said Marcos.

"We have to make sure that

he's back with his owner."

So, we rang the bell,

then ran back to the sidewalk.

A man came to the door.

"Is this your dog?" we called.

"No, he belongs to my brother,"

said the man, coming outside.

"I didn't even notice

he was missing!

Thank you for returning him."

"That's okay," we said,

and we went on our way.

"Did you see that man's ears?"

I asked.

"They were huge . . . and pointed!"

AFTERWORD

What idea do you think

Jamal had to save himself

at the end of *The Cousin?*

What did the three boys

do that was clever

after knocking at the man's door?

What would you do if you found

a lost dog?

WHERE THE STORIES COME FROM

Butterball is based on a story from Scandinavia. Similar stories, where a villain captures a child in a sack, can be found around the world.

The Lost Dog was inspired by a ghost story from Sierra Leone.

The Cousin has its origins in Iraq.